emoji death mask
poems or whatever

Johnny Kiosk

emoji death mask

Copyright © 2016 by Johnny Kiosk

ISBN-13: 978-0-9966595-4-3
ISBN-10: 0-9966595-4-4

www.maudlinhouse.net
www.twitter.com/maudlinhouse

P.O. Box 2015
Palatine, IL 60078

Printed in U.S.A.

television

tentacles of a giant firefly squid reach toward
my kitchen

peanut butter falls over

from the depths of the ocean the peanut butter
is sad

there is no news just the same things happening
over and over

television was invented by severely depressed
lonely people so they could watch the same
things happening over and over

people are amazed by the immense loneliness
of the depths of the ocean

a poster of a giant depressed squid

cats are the only pets that can adequately
handle depressed lonely people

cats
are the only pets
that can adequately
handle
**depressed
lonely
people**

twelve lonely people eating peanut butter and sushi in the middle of the afternoon on a tuesday

cats are reluctant to think the same things over and over

people watch the immense loneliness of the ocean on television over and over

a cat behind a refrigerator secretly eating sushi

there is a news report about a series of peanut butter related burglaries

a man is secretly screaming alone in the parking lot of a depressed sushi restaurant

cats sit on top of a television licking peanut butter off firefly squid tentacles while staring at severely depressed lonely people over and over

I am waiting for a new experience because all of the ones I've had suck.

I am only kind of depressed

I want to be ultra depressed

I want to lie in my bed for nine weeks and maybe eat a pretzel

and not care about the crumbs in my bed

I want to think about the single best moment in my life

then I will think about how this moment is gone

I will also think about how the other person in the moment is gone

I will ruminate philosophically on the fact that retroactively the best moment in my life is by far the worst moment in my life

it's pretty cool when you are depressed because
you get to remember beautiful moments that
are silently destroying you

moments that you block in day to day life so
you can function properly and go to school or
work.

I don't go to school or work.

I wonder how long I can make this last.

I feel like I need klonopin.

As far as the future is concerned from a
non-personal standpoint

I feel like computers will take over or we will
have a cataclysmic breakdown of the current
geopolitical climate

including our daily routines

either way it seems incredibly fucked

either way it seems unwise to have children

I kinda think most people don't think before
having children

I kinda think most people don't realize how
massive computers are in planning our day to
day lives.

Now that I've written a poem I will spend the
rest of the day sitting in my computer chair staring at lights on a screen

this is the future

the future will never hurt you

just kidding

bummer time mix #4

I sat on the sofa.

You sat on the sofa.

I watched anime.

You watched anime.

You cried when you thought the boy didn't get to the edge of the building in time to save the girl.

There were two cats and they kept getting in the way of the tv.

'I am tired of cats' I thought.

'These cats are funny' you said.

I walked to the kitchen to get another can of coke zero.

In the kitchen I stared at a large knife.

'Maybe I should stab myself.' I thought.

I thought first about stabbing my leg.

Then I thought about stabbing myself in the throat.

I accidentally pictured a cat being stabbed.

I felt bad about visualizing a cat being stabbed since it was not my intention to stab anything besides myself.

I figured if I stabbed myself in the throat after the first ten or so seconds shock would kick in

the loss of blood would probably create a sensation that resembles drifting off to sleep.

I came back from the kitchen.

'This is the last coke zero.'

'Can I have it?' you asked.

bummer time mix #3

I can't move anymore.

My bed is the extent of the physical universe.

I am fucked.

If you type it it can't be true.

Just kidding.

If you type it it's ultra true.

I want basically everyone I come into contact
with to leave me alone.

I wish everyone's faces had space bars.

'Go away' is my favorite expression.

If you punch enough holes in your wall you can
transcend yourself.

It is totally zen to punch inanimate objects.

schizoid apocalypse

I spend 160 hours a week in my room.

I do not leave my room unless it is after midnight so there are no people and only a few cars.

If I leave my room I walk around the lake listening to depressing ambient lo-fi drone shoegaze on my smartphone.

Sometimes I get tired of my room so I download Tosh.0 episodes

and laugh at people doing stupid things.

Then I feel better about my room.

Pretty much I don't want to be around people.

The thought of being around people makes me want to stab myself in the eye with an icepick.

But that would be impolite so I refrain from

stabbing myself.

If I was to commit suicide my suicide note would say:

"I'm sorry I killed myself.
Here is all the money I have.
Use it if you feel like having a funeral. Otherwise just keep it and do whatever.
Thanks."

i am severely alienated and i will use a word processor to convey emotions

i can clearly remember your face

and the black sunglasses you wore

and at least three of your shirts

and most of the bracelets

and bandanas you wore on your arms

but i can't put any of it into words

words would just shit on your beautiful face

words would poo on the memory of your shirts

fuck words

words can go to hell

or to nordstrom

and they can use a visa black card

on a POS system that is hacked
by russian anarchists

and their accounts can get emptied

and they can go home and lapse into severe
depression

because they realize they've lost everything

and will be unable to pay their mortgage

and will lose their insurance policies

and they will plan a painless suicide

involving large quantities of pills and a fifth of

vodka but they will become unconscious after

taking the pills and vomit up most of the pills

and be driven to a hospital

where they will have their stomachs pumped

but they won't make a full recovery

eventually they will be put on life support

and die an agonizing death over the course of 2-3 weeks.

jarhead emoji

I basically want my head to be removed sur-
gically with a laser beam that cauterizes the
bottom of my neck.

I don't want like veins dangling or anything
disgusting/gruesome.

Strange men with purple high-grade latex
gloves wearing hazmat suits typically reserved
for biohazard level 4 viral hemorrhagic diseases
will place my head in an airtight jar.

It will be like futurama only I will never talk or
cry.

Eventually I will forget how to blink and breathe.

I want your head to be removed

in a general non-violent manner

and placed in a jar next to my jar

we will be unable to communicate

or make eye contact

we will be unable to turn our heads

we will stare at a sterile white wall

for hundreds of years.

If I am capable of emotions

it might be a nice thought

the fact that your severed head

is next to my severed head.

email attachment

you are vague and amorphous
i am sadly always where i am
you left to have a life with a cat and a dog
i am still reading books
you are no longer vague and amorphous
you are beautiful and away
i read slowly and try to vanish
i become a bioluminescent jellyfish
that lacks the ability to glow
i swim down into darker waters with scarier fish
it is likely something terrifying will eat me
you sold shoes at the mall
while i checked the accuracy of google search
results i have at least nine books i want to send
you
you are in your bedroom petting your cat
i want to email myself to your bedroom

protip

it feels good to quit

i am waiting gleefully for the end so i can quit

everything at once

various places

feeling thoughtless

feeling like a cactus wearing an emotional
sweater

when it comes to moods and psychological
states

feel like i should be sad

i should be the saddest text message in the
world

regarding my lack of emotional states

feel like i should live in a colder city

and feel like a warm fuzzy tired void wearing a
scarf drinking coffee reading depressing novels
and Heidegger

feeling empty frozen and ok in a way that
implies i am accepting everything as it is and i

cannot change anything other than my thoughts

and even my thoughts i can only sort of change

so i will just accept them and acknowledge that
pain is permanent yet transitory like all things
in life except death and emails from the mail-
er-daemon

in the colder city i walk to a bridge

and stare at ice floating in the river

i send you the saddest text message in the
world

i jump from the bridge

and land on a piece of ice

and i float to the arctic circle

where depressed polar bears teach me how to
cry

they build an igloo

and we cry late at night

but since it is winter in the arctic circle

night lasts all day

so the polar bears and narwhals and i cry

for weeks at a time

when we cry our tears immediately freeze

our tears fall to the ground in tiny heart shapes

with their tusks the narwhals shatter the frozen

tiny heart shaped tears

the narwhals say 'fuck hearts'

the narwhals make the existential decision to

start listening to death metal and stop feeling
emotional

as a result of global warming the glacier we're
on melts and i float back to america and i can't
cry anymore

in public libraries i search for your name online

i travel to various arid regions

and write secret poems behind cacti

i pull a needle off a cactus and stab my arm

and write a secret poem with my blood in the
sand

'your poem is dumb' says the cactus

'i know' i say 'that's why i wrote it in the sand

away from people'

'they will never publish it'

'i don't care' i say while secretly caring

'you should just cover it up with more sand'

'maybe. i don't know.' i say

'it's pretty melodramatic to write a poem with
your blood. just cover it up.' says the cactus

i move to another cactus and write a shorter
different poem

i feel like the first cactus would be less critical of
this poem

desert animals are unhelpful in my doomed
and masochistic quest to locate your new email

our tears fall to the ground in tiny heart shapes

with their tusks the narwhals shatter the frozen

tiny heart shaped tears

the narwhals say 'fuck hearts'

the narwhals make the existenial

decision to start listening to death metal

and stop feeling

emotional

address

the desert animals say 'chill. just scope the awe-
some constellations'

i say 'the constellations are cool'

but really i don't think that i just lied to be polite
to the desert animals

due to severe depression, low self-esteem and
anhedonia i don't care about stars or nature

while they are looking at the stars

i leave and travel to various geographic regions

places where i don't have to hear people

places where i can privately perform depressing

google searches quoting things you said to me

in the past

there are no search results

i fall asleep beside a rock

I am at your house watching Straw Dogs circa 2005

I want you to boil water
I tell you it's for tea
'The water is boiling' you say
'Ok good. Pour it on my face.'
I am thinking of that Dustin Hoffman movie
where he is a mathematician or an astronomer
or something and he pours scalding water on
british thugs
I want to be your british thug
I want you to be my Dustin Hoffman
you say 'No, I won't pour this on you.'
you sound indignant
you are super attractive when you're indignant
I say 'Why, it makes perfect sense, like in that
movie.'
I want you to have stronger feelings about me
this includes the possibility of hatred
basically I am all or nothing so you need
to love me insanely, so insanely that you
would pour hot water on me so that my
grossly disfigured face would turn off possible
competitors and only belong to you
who would take care of me and love me

despite my grotesque face
which shows your magnanimity and uncondi-
tional love
or I want you to hate me so much that
you pour boiling water on my face
just to ruin me and to ensure that I can
never be happy again
that every time I look in the mirror
I will remember when I had a normal face
and you had a beautiful face

**i feel extremely alienated from all forms of
existence which means i cannot sleep since
i am sitting awake in the dark chewing my
fingernails as a passive-aggressive way
to lash out at all forms of existence while
telling myself 'don't think about how fucked
you are, don't think about time' while trying
to read an ebook of kokoro**

the future is fucked

the present is fucked

the past will be fucked

tomorrow i will envy today

which i currently hate

and which i recognize is fucked

i want to pet my cat

but he is outside my room

if i think about my life or my friendships

i want to die

most comedians are depressed

charles rocket slit his throat alone in a field

if i could be an animal i might be a bison

i'd live at yellowstone and wolves would eventually kill me

maybe i'd be a dust mite instead

or something invisible that lives on human skin

i suck at decisions

i feel like every decision is an attempt to stop
myself from thinking about death

death is decided for us

i will go think about what kind of coffin my rela-
tives will pick for me

just kidding

the point of life is to not think about life

emotional research grants

i want every street corner to be full of people waiting to cross the street

i want each person waiting to cross the street to be waiting to cross the street because they saw their ex on the other side of the street

once the person has started crossing the street

i want the ex gf/bf to walk away from the person

i want the ex gf/bf to never face the person

i would also like every solar system to collapse in on itself and form immense black holes that absorb all meaningful information from the universe

i want light pollution to severely interfere with migratory birds up to the point of mass extinction

i want darpa to invest more money into research

projects that figure out how to make humans
feel even more like shit

i want darpa to build a slow death ray gun that
makes everyone depressed and want to stay in
bed all the time

cover letter

I do not remember dreams
most of the time I sleep for at least 12 hours
in the morning I push my velleity
out through the slits in my ribcage sort of like
one dollar bills coming out of an atm
and slowly peel myself from my bed like a crane
lifting a 1984 chevy impala that was driven off
a cliffside and exploded like it was in
one of those nic cage movies at redbox that you
didn't even know was a movie

haiku

let cats have space/time
this will make it easier
to move on with life

vengeful emoji

you said i am experiencing neurological altering
emotions

i said i can only experience emotions if they're
filtered through a novel

you said move to colorado

i said i am broke

you sent me a picture of a tiny dragon

you said most things resolve themselves while i
pretend i didn't see them

you said i want to run away and live in the
mountains and watch depressing movies while
dipping gluten free crackers in box wine

i said i want your face to touch my face in a way
that implies the final moment of the universe

i am motionless in my room between towers of

depressed and manic books thinking of our chat
logs

you were alone in colorado the night i felt a
silent emotion that i wanted to express but
couldn't because i didn't have your new phone
number or email address

to convey your anger i want you to do something extremely violent and unique and previ-
ously unthought of to my body

i would rather have you chop me into one inch
cubes and store them in a box in your attic until
a cat discovers the box and devours the cubes
than to never talk again

i want your anger to turn into a sledgehammer
and shatter my sternum and then you disas-
semble my heart and play jenga with the pieces
while you laugh and throw saltine wrappers on
my corpse and light my corpse on fire using box
wine and vodka as fuel

i want you to crush me into a giant ball and roll
me down a mountain where i will gain momen-
tum and smash into a tree

and knock the tree over

creating a domino effect of trees until there is
a treeless line in the middle of a giant forest
where bears will chase hikers for hundreds of
miles

until the hikers reach a freeway and flag down
an eighteen wheeler

and just when the hikers feel safe a bear will
pop out like in a horror movie and kill the hikers
and truck driver

the next century

i am an idiot who likes

to stare at a screen for 14 hours

straight and has lost interest

in body parts

even reproductive organs

i think there will be no

more ok times

it's only bummer times

and that's cool

quantum tragic

almost.

existential ramen

Instead of thinking about talking or thinking I will boil water.

I will pour boiling water over ramen.

I might eat the noodles.

I wish it would rain for 1,000 years.

Through the window of an unlighted kitchen

I stare at a silver leaf maple tree.

Steam rises from a cup of ramen.

I think about dying.

I feel ok.

Non-committal emoji

You were born on a different planet.
You have purple hair frequently.
You have two cats that practice backflips and
tableleaps.
I was born on the planet where you sit in a com-
puter chair for ten hours a day.
The planet I was born on is diagnosed with
bipolar and schizoid.
Your planet orbits two suns and is moody as
fuck but sometimes has
          a really nice springtime when it is at the
proper distance from both suns.
Your planet has really low selfesteem.
My planet punches itself in the face.

a place where i am not

i would like to move away

or at least rearrange my room and

pretend i've moved away.

Romantic emoticon

We were at a friend's birthday party
he gave everyone ecstasy
I started freaking out because I had read on
wikipedia about possible deleterious side ef-
fects to the brain
some guy tried to calm me down and told me
to drink water
a girl from austin who I had talked to on face-
book was there
she approached me in the pool and started
rubbing me
she said she wanted to fuck me
I got nervous and looked to my group of friends
I told her I liked another girl at the party
the other girl said she liked me too
she said she would give me a ride home
then I said 'I will also give you a ride home'
which doesn't make much sense
the girl from austin left the party
she fell asleep in a ditch
I felt pretty bad
the other girl and I lied on the sofa and I traded
her my shirt for her panties now we have been
together for three years

the future is inside some top secret quantum computer

computers will ingest the future

this is a known fact

numerology is an extensive pseudo scientific

field it along with advanced mathematics

ensures we will die

alone in our bedrooms

in some gutter of a futuristic city

beside a tree

on a mountain

somewhere

anywhere

I lie on the floor hyperventilating

and punching myself

in the emoji.

tips and tricks

I lie on the floor hyperventilating and punching myself in the emoji.

c y b e r p o e m

i am aware of the carpet under my feet

this makes me feel new age

i don't want to feel new age

so i will look at online pictures of soviet russia

or the berlin wall

or hiroshima

or other things that are responsible for

our cultural amnesia

not really

nothing is responsible for anything

so everyone is fully responsible for their

own behavior and all of their

decisions including buying a big mac or

shamwow because they saw a commercial

they don't consciously remember a long time

ago that's dumb.

instead i will imagine being a cyberpunk wizard

gandalf with a skrillex haircut

a nano nucleonic chronomancer

a time wizard to be precise.

yes, i am a time wizard.

to prove this, i wear a smartwatch at all times

except when i am not wearing it, at which time
Time stops.

that means i am a time wizard.

time hacks everything.

time illegally downloads everything and then
slowly deletes it.

i am having a time crisis.

my thoughts are as ocd as the hands of a clock.

the soul is not bioluminescent.

i refuse to go shopping in a world

in which trees are becoming bioluminescent.

call this a cyber poem.

i am influenced by music.

i am listening to perturbator

so i can feel cyberpunk.

the heart is a darknet.

cyberpunk is dirty, but sophisticated,

i like my girls cyberpunk

because i am a rat

i desire to live in the sewers.

i see all the desires of your asynchronous

distributed mesh network.

your panopticon

& the eye of God.

fear is the future.

the future is a terrorist.

time will go Ozymandias on us.

it's cyberpunk to be ocd

it's definitely cyberpunk to be paranoid.

be paranoid of emoticons.

be as paranoid of emotions

as tiny rabbits are afraid

of weaponized hawks.

friendship is definitely suspect.

everything is money.

money is nothing.

your networks suck.

everything is a network.

death is what everyone wants to buy.

death is always sold for more money than you
could possibly have.

everything sucks and it is all available as a tor-
rent.

this has been a cyber poem.

if there is a future, it will seem quaint.

neutral face emoji

i am on the other side of my death
peering through my eyes
disinterestedly watching my life
like a made for tv movie

other planets

i will disappear
into the blue screen of death
i will become a windows 95 screensaver
you will see an endless succession of stars
you will feel awe at the massive scope of the
universe
i will become a printer on sale at best buy
you will tell your husband and children
you will feel awe at the great savings
i will disappear
i will become some planet
that lacks information technology
i will just sit there orbiting
binary stars with
rocks or maybe trees
pine trees
i will be cold and alone
and i will feel awe

graveside emoticon

On my tombstone

I want it to read:

:P

insane russian and american scientists are secretly creating a massive existential crisis

a piece of paper in the mail says, 'where are your taxes?'

i say 'i've sent them'

the paper grabs my head and slaps me

'i want the truth' it says

i throw the paper out the window

the paper gets in one of those black fbi suvs and drives away

if i was going to do something insane i would have done it by now

i am really good at procrastination

procrastination is the first thing i do in the morning

i am going to grab an empty jar of peanut butter out of the trash and scrape out the residual
peanut butter and make a sandwich with my last
piece of expired bread and feel satisfied

i will write you an email later

eventually i will buy bananas

i have between fifty and two hundred dollars
stashed under my bed

i am going to read novels for five hours

but later

i walk to a bar and stare at a homeless man
outside the bar

i imagine him using magic or advanced technology to download people's credit card information from their smartphones and redistributing
the credit card numbers to other homeless people and underpaid construction workers who will
buy milkshakes from whataburger unafraid of
bill payments

there is a smiley face on a giant banner on a
new high rise

my life is pointless
i read that in a book once

some people are picketing the high rise

some people give long monologues on the eco-
logical and moral hazards of high rises

some people with megaphones say high rises
will take the mystery and challenge out of life

a man applauds fervently, compassionately

someone chants 'the high rise will destroy our
lives'

i try to determine if that's iambic

the number of people in the world should be
illegal

the number of people in the world necessitates
illegally tall high rises

other people are paying their taxes

i wonder if we dye all the tax money glow-in-
the-dark can we see where it goes

secret things are happening in massive subter-
ranean complexes involving sharks and toxic
waste

massive insane things are occurring on a never
before seen scale in top secret labs involving
weaponized pine trees, mind-controlled dol-
phins and the cross breeding of rats and octopi

new technologies must be designed for global
warfare otherwise tv ratings would drop

when tv ratings drop people go outside and
that is considered a threat

i get another letter in the mail

it is a formal letter letting me know my reading
habits are wiretapped

the president wants to know what book i am
currently reading and if my reading habits pose
an existential threat to humanity or taxpayers

i want to eat eight bananas

my life is pointless

i read that in a book once

bummer time mix #5

this poem is the result of massive

indifference

which means I've basically run out of things

which means moods

or meaningful life events

or interesting documentaries

or cat gifs

or pictures of siberian forests from images.
google.com

or insane experiences with cybernetics

which reduce my biologically derived

psychological states to an experiment

a failed experiment that resulted in the

ability to write certain statements

which are meant to inflict more

statements on my consciousness

until I have a nervous breakdown/yearn for first
order feelings

that include something present, concrete and
positive in a relevant and impactful way

or at least a well-formed memory involving

a face with concrete details

like an eye of a certain color

or a specific facial contour

or maybe a tone of voice

all my memories are meta

like the faint glow of a lamp that you

never look directly at but can tell it's in

the room because of the green reflection of its

lampshade in your eyeglasses

my memories are spectral

all my memories have sublimated into plasma

and dance on my window panes like solar flares

that I avoid looking at

haiku

Bury me with a
smartphone. I want to live tweet
from beyond the grave.

How to dephase oneself via downcycling quantum emotional and molecular states

First you realize you no longer have emotions, just vague and blunted fight-or-flight response mechanisms.
Next you realize you have no opinions, just references to other people's opinions and blogs.
After that you realize you can no longer go for walks.
Even if you do go for a walk you won't enjoy it.

twenty thousand light years

i have a time machine

it is called my bed

when i close my eyes for long periods of time

i wake up in the future

you are wearing a jack o lantern shirt

you eat chocolate cereal with marshmallows for dinner

you feed a cage of domesticated rats

you have bestowed civilized personalities on rats

if i talk long enough i can avoid having to express empathy

you say what if i was a rat

i say i would feed you chocolate cereal with
marshmallows

you are an intergalactic freeway made of stars
and galaxies

along your highways there are nebulae and
solar flares

occasionally there is an extraterrestrial homeworld

and the extraterrestrials generally ignore my
emotional states

i pass by their homeworld with a blank facial
expression

i feel depressed, happy and abandoned

watching cosmic spirals flashing around binary
star systems

on my spaceship there are pine trees

the pine trees provide oxygen and life
support

in the trees are squirrels

they throw pinecones at the fragile posi-
tron-based machinery that powers the warp
engines

the squirrels make tiny laughing sounds

the ship veers out of control

the ship explodes

i drift toward a black hole

i stretch and swirl into nothingness

i smile near the event horizon

i become an eternal emoji

you continue on for 20,000 light years

wearing a purple sweater you avoid the coldest
regions of space

you want to leave behind the stacks of catalogs
and unanswered letters you've received over
the past year

you want to forget about cleaning out your
refrigerator or dishwasher

you drift through space for thousands of years

eventually you find a super earth with better
geographic regions

you reside there among the rats and waves

a new sun is shining for a while you don't think
about dying

the bridge

You wanted to walk at the park
we drove to the park 'there are too many peo-
ple' I said
we drove around for forty minutes
looking at the sky and artificial lakes
'I want to walk' you said.
I drove to Randall's.
I parked the car.
We got out and walked on the sidewalk beside
the bayou.
We didn't talk much.
We stared at dead trees.
We looked at a broken piece of sidewalk that
had 'Ants <--' spray painted in blue.
While taking a picture of a dead tree I stepped
in an ant bed.
You swatted a fire ant off my shoe.
You pointed out electrical boxes that had been
graffitied to look like giant robot faces.
You noticed the way the setting sun lined a
huge cloud with gold.
I took pictures of new spy equipment the police
department had installed on a telephone pole.

We stood on the bridge.
I took a picture of you.
You tried not to smile 'I am trying not to smile.
I want the picture to look real.' you said.
Behind you the golden clouds were disappear-
ing.

haiku

every day is a
new day this fact fucking bores
me infinitely

disappearing emoji

my cat is eating a plastic bag

i try to pet his tail but he rotates away from me
while keeping his mouth on the plastic bag

a digital clock spits in my eyes

i am going to eat twenty cookies while taking a
nap

it is 3 am

there is more life in my web browser than in my
life

the complexity of the refrigerator is staggering

the staggering complexity of the refrigerator is
making me read ancient philosophy

the complexity of self destructive enzymes dis-
solving hair clogs is mind-destroying

self destructive enzymes are making me send
mass text messages

it is 2 am

reading kant fast enough to melt my brain

i try to paint vivid landscapes of noumena

the refrigerator is making distant forlorn sounds

there is not enough paint in the world to repre-
sent the negative emotional states i am experiencing

if you really love someone you will leave them
alone

because it is impossible to be close to someone
without gently crushing them beneath your will

my cat is hiding in a plastic bag

it is 4 am

in distant locations people are covering their
ears

my cat is floating away inside a tiny plastic bag

there are empty sounds coming out of my head

i am alone inside a shiny vortex

i can feel every emotion to an insane degree
but only if i'm copying it from a movie

haiku

there are things that seem
to matter eventually
they stop mattering

sky poem

The sky talks shit about its friends,

then passive-aggressively retweets their most
and least popular tweets.

The sky is bipolar.

The sky has generalized anxiety disorder.

The sky has experienced psychotic depression.

The sky realizes that in the past people didn't
have diagnosable psychological disorders to
get worked up over and instead could focus on
writing long books.

Often these long books were attributed not to
the idiosyncratic genius of the author, but to the
fates or Fate or the gods or God, which alleviat-
ed lots of creative induced stress.

The sky does not know if it believes in god,
though it frequently considers this urge to be

more worth its time than glibly accepting materialism, which seems to tacitly hinge on non-materialistic ontological underpinnings.

The sky almost feels like today's popularized scientism is effectively a cultural mythos that has replaced the knowledge that paradise cannot exist on earth with the insanity that technology can only make things better.

The sky thinks it is dumb.

The sky stares at itself in the mirror and recites dream song 14.

The sky covers itself with dark gray blankets of clouds, changes its gchat status to invisible, drinks some benadryl and stares at the random shapes in the stucco ceiling, pretending they are cloud formations.

incorporeal emoji

pretty much feel like a ghost

a cartoon ghost

that can be hit by doors

when people without incorporeality swing them
open

to leave & go places

bummer time mix #2

there is nothing i'd like more
than to be dying
alone in a field
to feel the wind and see the clouds
and hear the rustling of tall grass

annihilation emoji

after 5000 books you will level up
after 20,000 cups of tea you will gain +2 to
wisdom
after 7 billion people on earth the internet of
things will eat your children
i will decapitate myself to prove how insufficient
my emotions are in terms of making someone
feel ok when confronted with the possibility of
imminent death or eventual death
i feel paralyzed when I am forced to think about
the ontological status of love or when i have to
make decisions about long-term relationships or
even just jobs
i will avoid my problems by reading depressing
novels
i will have panic attacks while watching tv or
movies
to combat extreme lethargy and depressive
thoughts i consume at least 500 mg of caffeine
a day
caffeine increases my anxiety at least thirty times
my caffeinated anxiety is a juggernaut/ancient
greek cyclops that decimates metropolitan

i feel happy when i feel shitty

thanks

skylines and annihilates low orbit satellites
my caffeinated anxiety feels like four billion tiny
electric cats wearing jetpacks fist fighting in my
bloodstream
i feel happy when i feel shitty
thanks

THE AUTHOR

Johnny Kiosk lives, sleeps, and checks his email in or near Houston. Sometimes he rides a bike.